What Makes a SUPERSTAR ATHLETE?

James Roland

San Diego, CA

© 2023 ReferencePoint Press, Inc.
Printed in the United States

For more information, contact:
ReferencePoint Press, Inc.
PO Box 27779
San Diego, CA 92198
www.ReferencePointPress.com

ALL RIGHTS RESERVED.
No part of this work covered by the copyright hereon may be reproduced or used in any form or by any means—graphic, electronic, or mechanical, including photocopying, recording, taping, web distribution, or information storage retrieval systems—without the written permission of the publisher.

LIBRARY OF CONGRESS CATALOGING-IN-PUBLICATION DATA

Names: Roland, James, author.
Title: What makes a superstar athlete? / By James Roland.
Description: San Diego, CA : ReferencePoint Press, Inc. [2023] | Includes bibliographical references and index.
Identifiers: LCCN 2022037127 (print) | LCCN 2022037128 (ebook) | ISBN 9781678204846 (library binding) | ISBN 9781678204853 (ebook)
Subjects: LCSH: Athletes--Training of--Juvenile literature. | Athletes--Mental health--Juvenile literature. | Sports--Physiological aspects--Juvenile literature. | Teamwork (Sports)--Juvenile literature.
Classification: LCC GV711.5 .R65 2023 (print) | LCC GV711.5 (ebook) | DDC 613.7/11--dc23/eng/20220811
LC record available at https://lccn.loc.gov/2022037127
LC ebook record available at https://lccn.loc.gov/2022037128

CONTENTS

Introduction   4
A Superstar in the Making

Chapter One   8
Maximizing Potential

Chapter Two   19
Mental Toughness

Chapter Three   30
Superstar Support

Chapter Four   41
Seizing Opportunities

Source Notes	53
Organizations and Websites	57
For Further Research	58
Index	59
Picture Credits	63
About the Author	64

INTRODUCTION

A Superstar in the Making

Long before he became one of the most exciting superstars in the National Basketball Association (NBA), Stephen Curry set out on the path that would ultimately lead him to the top of his sport. In a rec league basketball game in his hometown of Charlotte, North Carolina, six-year-old Steph raced down the court on a fast break with one other teammate. When a player on the other team started guarding him, young Steph opted to pass the ball to his teammate. But rather than make a simple bounce pass or chest pass, he jumped in the air and turned around, flinging the ball behind his back. That is the moment the 2022 NBA Finals Most Valuable Player (MVP) says he decided on a career in basketball. In recalling the pass and the reaction of the parents in the bleachers, Curry wrote in the online journal Players' Tribune, "It was right on target, and my teammate, he laid it up. And all 15 fans in the crowd went crazy. And, obviously, it was pretty beauty. But that was the moment that my creativity kind of came out and I knew there was going to be that type of reaction. So, I knew at that point that basketball was fun for me and I loved to do it, so . . . that was it."[1]

Working Hard to Be the Best

These days Curry makes sensational plays before thousands of people in packed arenas and millions more watching on TV.

He may be the greatest shooter in NBA history, as he holds the record for most career three-pointers and the most three-pointers made in a single season. He also holds the Golden State Warriors' all-time team record for points and assists, and he is the only player in NBA history to be unanimously selected for the MVP Award.

But there is more to his game than the flashy creativity and long-range shooting skills fans see during the games. Like most superstar athletes with long careers, Curry works hard at his sport all year round when there are no cameras or screaming fans anywhere in sight. He and his trainer, Brandon Payne, come up with a long list of running and shooting drills that Curry works through during the season and in the off-season.

In fact, he is considered one of the hardest-working athletes in his profession. For example, he takes around two thousand jump shots every week and has been doing that and more since he was a child. "He enjoys it so much and he loves the process. That's one of the things that ties all great athletes together," Golden State Warriors coach Steve Kerr says of his remarkable point guard. "There's a routine that not only is super-disciplined, but it's really enjoyed each day. There's a passion that comes with it, and that's what sustains it over time. When you love something like those guys do, you work at it, you get better and you just keep going."[2]

Having a Desire to Succeed and the Support of Others

Along with putting in countless hours of practice and enjoying the rewards that endeavor brings, Curry and most superstar athletes also have a shared mental approach to their sports. They have a toughness and confidence that matches their physical strength and skill. They start with a burning desire to be the best in their sport and a belief that they can indeed become a superstar. As

Curry's Warriors teammate Draymond Green said in an interview with the website Stack:

> Before you can ever reach anything you have to believe it. You don't just mistakenly become great at something—you probably at one time or another believed that you could be great at that. And then you worked to get great at that and you reached that greatness. But you don't mistakenly become great and then you start to believe "Oh man, I'm great at that!" No, you believed that before and you worked to get that. So I always believe that and I work every day to reach that.[3]

Yet these great athletes do not attain greatness alone. The superstars in team sports are usually supported by teammates who help the stars win championships and perform to their potential. The superstars in individual sports, such as snowboarding and tennis, may not have teammates, but they have coaches, trainers, and others in their orbit helping them improve their skills and fitness and making sure they can excel year after year.

More than Just Talent

It is not just having talent and a talented supporting cast that allows an athlete to become a superstar. Sports legends also seem to have a knack for playing at their best when a championship or other prize is on the line—even if it means channeling some nervous energy into their performance. "I've never been afraid of big moments. I get butterflies," Curry says. "I get nervous and anxious, but I think those are all good signs that I'm ready for the moment."[4]

Being ready for the moment often distinguishes superstars from other tal-

> "Before you can ever reach anything you have to believe it. You don't just mistakenly become great at something."[3]
>
> —Draymond Green, professional basketball player

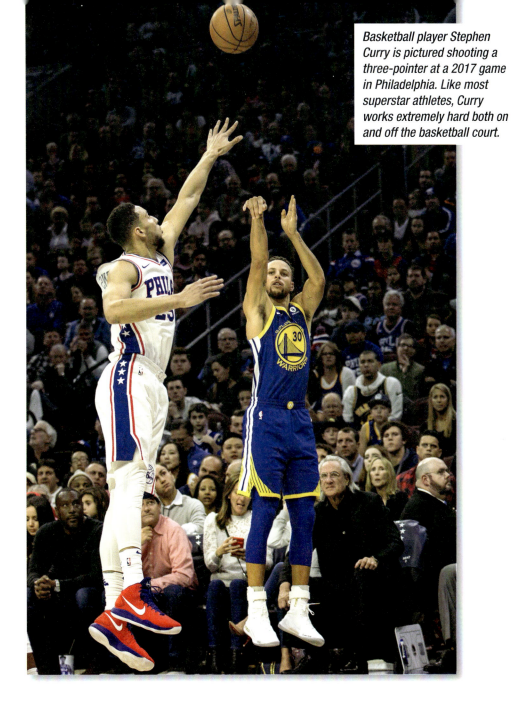

Basketball player Stephen Curry is pictured shooting a three-pointer at a 2017 game in Philadelphia. Like most superstar athletes, Curry works extremely hard both on and off the basketball court.

ented players. Superstar athletes rise to each challenge and perform well under pressure. They practice for greatness. And when the opportunity to shine comes, they put that practice into action and enjoy each moment, knowing they have worked hard to become the best.

CHAPTER ONE

Maximizing Potential

Superstar athletes literally come in all shapes and sizes. Two of America's greatest Olympians of all time—gymnast Simone Biles and swimmer Michael Phelps—stand four feet eight inches (4'8") and six feet four inches (6'4"), respectively. But what Biles, Phelps, and the superstars in every sport all have in common is that they take whatever natural gifts or talents they were born with and devote endless hours to perfecting their skills and working out to improve their strength, flexibility, and endurance. Until a superstar athlete retires, it is a never-ending process that can be both a physical and mental struggle at times. But in the end, the results can be breathtaking.

Biles learned to launch her compact, mighty body into dazzling routines that earned her gold medals, world records, and the admiration of fans around the world, especially young girls who want to give gymnastics or other sports a try. "It's amazing that I can inspire little kids to know that you can be short or tall and your body type doesn't matter because you can do anything,"[5] she told *Women's Health* magazine.

Phelps, with his long arms and flipper-like feet, took a body built for swimming and became the most decorated athlete in Olympic history. He and his fellow superstars could have had moderate success in their sports without putting in countless hours of training. But like others who ascend to greatness, they were not satisfied with a decent career. They chose the hard road to get them to the top of their sports.

Harvard track-and-field coach Kebba Tolbert, who helped sprinter Gabby Thomas become a two-time medalist in the 2021 Olympics, told *Harvard Magazine* that natural talent can be a blessing and a curse. "The blessing is, you can achieve at a high level. The curse is that sometimes you don't realize all the work it's going to take to get to the next level, because the level you're at came fairly easy,"[6] Tolbert said.

Getting to the Next Level

To get to that next level, superstars train hard, eat healthy foods, get plenty of sleep, and manage their thoughts and emotions so they do not get distracted or discouraged. They practice the

Gymnast Simone Biles is one of America's greatest Olympians of all time. Here, she performs her floor routine at the 2019 Artistic Gymnastics World Championships in Stuttgart, Germany. Her dedication and skill have inspired fans around the world.

fundamentals of their sport all year round. And they do all this with the attitude that they can get better if they just keep working hard and look for strategies to elevate their game. Even the athletes who reach the pinnacles of their sports keep working to find ways to improve. They see a direct connection between success and exhaustive workouts and grueling practice sessions.

Just a few months after leading his team to the Super Bowl LIV title in 2020, Kansas City Chiefs quarterback Patrick Mahomes was hard at work in the middle of a steaming-hot summer in Texas with his longtime trainer, Bobby Stroupe. Together they were coming up with a new workout routine that would improve both Mahomes's flexibility and arm strength. "I had to find a way to make myself better," Mahomes told *Men's Health* magazine. "It's trying to find the next step."[7]

For Mahomes, a typical two-hour workout might include forty short, medium, and long passes from a variety of angles, as well as twenty-three different exercises that cover all major muscle groups. "I just always wanted to find a way to be on top at the end of the day," says Mahomes. "I was able to do that early in my career. And I'm gonna try to continue to get back to that feeling again."[8]

> "I just always wanted to find a way to be on top at the end of the day. I was able to do that early in my career. And I'm gonna try to continue to get back to that feeling again."[8]
>
> —Patrick Mahomes, NFL quarterback

Choosing the Right Sport

Many superstar athletes play multiple sports when they are young but ultimately choose one in which to concentrate all their efforts. That decision can make the difference between becoming a legend in one sport or an average athlete in a different sport. For some, it is a matter of picking the sport they enjoyed the most or the one that seemed most likely to allow them to fulfill childhood dreams of sports success.

Setting Goals for Success

Sports success may seem like it is all about split-second decision-making and amazing athletic skill. And while those factors are certainly part of the equation, most superstars reach the top by setting specific goals and working toward them day after day, year after year. Starting at a young age, many superstars keep a record of their goals and accomplishments and visualize a future in which they achieve at the highest levels. While in high school and college, Aidan Hutchinson, an all-American defensive lineman at the University of Michigan and an NFL first-round draft pick in 2022, kept a nightly journal of his goals, thoughts, and visions of future success. He believed so strongly in visualizing specific accomplishments that on the night his name was called in the NFL draft, he took the stage to meet NFL commissioner Roger Goodell in a suit that his mother had made for him with dozens of messages from his journals embroidered on the inside of the jacket. "Stuff like, 'I'm going to be a first-team All-American,' 'I'm going to be a Heisman finalist,' and you know, a lot of that stuff came true," he told ESPN reporter Melissa Stark after he was drafted by the Detroit Lions.

Quoted in Tony Garcia, "Detroit Lions' Aidan Hutchinson Got His Start in Dance: 4 Things to Know About Him," *Detroit Free Press*, April 28, 2022. www.freep.com.

Growing up in Connecticut, US Olympic snowboard cross champion Lindsey Jacobellis skied and snowboarded in the winter, played softball when the snow melted in the spring, and spent autumn afternoons playing field hockey. And whenever she got a spare minute, she, her brother, and their friends skateboarded around the neighborhood. "My parents put me into sports and I was always playing outside with my brother," she said in an interview with outdoor adventure website the Clymb. "Every season my brother and I would be involved in a sport that ranged from swimming, softball/baseball, lacrosse, field hockey, skiing, snowboarding and skateboarding."[9] It was not until winning local snowboard cross events in high school led her to national competition and then the international Grand Prix circuit that she made snowboarding her number one priority.

Kyler Murray was also a multisport athlete as a kid. The Texas native became a standout high school baseball and football player, attracting many college scouts to his games in both sports. He continued to play both sports at a high level at the University of Oklahoma, winning college football's Heisman Trophy as an all-American quarterback and being a first-round draft pick by the Oakland Athletics in baseball. Ultimately, Murray opted for a career in football, quickly becoming a budding superstar after being drafted by the Arizona Cardinals in 2019. "Picking football over baseball was one of the hardest decisions I've ever had to make," Murray told *GQ* magazine. "For me personally, I grew up wanting to win Super Bowls. I always watched the Super Bowl. I knew everything about the game still, you know. So it was for me personally, like I said, it was just something about the game of football that I love."[10]

For other superstars, their physical attributes guided their decision. NBA Hall of Famer Hakeem Olajuwon was a standout soccer goalkeeper growing up in Lagos, Nigeria. But by the time he was fifteen years old, he stood six feet nine inches tall and decided to give basketball a try at the urging of youth basketball coaches in his community. A few years later Olajuwon led the University of Houston men's basketball team to back-to-back National Collegiate Athletic Association (NCAA) championship games. After that, he starred on the Houston Rockets' two NBA title winners and went on to be selected to the NBA Hall of Fame. Like many superstar athletes who switch sports, Olajuwon used what he had learned in one sport and applied it to the other. "All my fakes in basketball are from soccer," he told the *Los Angeles Times*. "It's body movement, footwork. That was my foundation to be agile for my height."[11]

Travis Cooper, who grew up in Georgia playing just about every sport he could, also changed sports when he realized his body might not be suited to the ones he loved most. His favorites were baseball and football. He also wrestled and lifted weights to get stronger for the other sports. But at five feet five inches tall in high school, he decided to narrow his athletic pursuits. "I realized that I was never going to be tall enough or big enough to be a successful football or baseball player, so I decided to concentrate on wrestling,"[12] he said in an interview with Catalyst Athletics. But he also kept lifting weights and was soon outlifting his bigger, taller peers in the weight room. Eventually, he dropped wrestling to focus full time on weight lifting—a decision that eventually led him to become a three-time US champion.

Staying in Shape

No matter how athletes are built or what sports they choose, they can always improve their strength, agility, and athletic skills. And the superstars are often some of the most dedicated individuals when it comes to staying in shape and staying competitive.

Tom Brady, who has won more Super Bowls than any other National Football League (NFL) player, is famous for his off-season workout routine, which includes six to seven days a week of cardio

Quarterback Tom Brady takes a knee during an August 2022 practice. Brady is famous for his off-season routine, which helps him continually improve his game.

> "My college coach used to say, 'Better or worse: What's it gonna be?' I love to learn and to see improvement."[13]
>
> —Tom Brady, NFL quarterback

workouts and a mix of resistance band exercises, weight lifting, Pilates, and a strict diet that includes little unhealthy food. He even opts for avocado ice cream because it is healthier than traditional flavors like chocolate.

Like many superstars who have had long careers, Brady knows that varying his workouts and trying new things keeps him mentally focused and helps his body avoid repetitive motion injuries. "I love the game, and I always want to improve," Brady told the Bleacher Report website. "My college coach used to say, 'Better or worse: What's it gonna be?' I love to learn and to see improvement."[13]

While every sport has a unique set of demands, most require a certain amount of strength, speed, flexibility, and endurance. For two-time Olympic snowboarding gold medalist Chloe Kim, part of her training obviously involves strapping on her snowboard and practicing her routines. But over the course of an entire year, more time is spent on strength training and conditioning. "My training routine's pretty crazy," she told *Shape* magazine, explaining that she works out nearly every day so that her "body can sustain the impact from falling."[14] Kim does a lot of heavy lifting and exercises that work one leg at a time. When exercising both legs at the same time, it is possible to "cheat" and favor one leg, which results in one leg being stronger than the other. She also runs, which allows her to spend time outdoors during the warm weather months. Of exercising, Kim says, "It's definitely helped me improve my snowboarding, so that's why I do it."[15]

But for top athletes, it is not just about working up a sweat and pushing their body to the limits. In recent years, scientists have learned just how critical sleep is for health and how elite athletes in particular have to prioritize sleep in order to let their bodies recover from those grueling workouts. Women's National Basketball Association (WNBA) champion and Olympic gold medal basketball player Sue Bird told *SELF* magazine that getting enough sleep not only helps the body but is vital to reducing the stress that comes with competition. "A lot of taking care of my body means making sure I'm getting enough sleep, and recovery is a big part of that," Bird said. "The better sleep you get, the better recovered you'll be."[16]

> "A lot of taking care of my body means making sure I'm getting enough sleep, and recovery is a big part of that. The better sleep you get, the better recovered you'll be."[16]
>
> —Sue Bird, WNBA star

Skills Training

Conditioning certainly helps superstars stay in top physical shape and reduce the risk of injury. But to remain at the top of their game, superstars spend countless hours on the fundamental skills unique to their sports. This is why Major League Baseball players take batting practice and fielding practice before every game. It is also why basketball players take hundreds of shots

Most superstar athletes spend hours working on fundamental skills. For instance, Major League Baseball players take batting and fielding practice before every game. This picture shows Boston Red Sox hitter J.D. Martinez at batting practice before a 2019 game.

every week and why Olympic divers practice the same dives over and over again. It is often said of the top athletes in any sport that they are the first ones to show up for practice and the last ones to leave.

To stay motivated to work on the same skills day after day, year after year, some superstars come up with creative ways of approaching practice. Some athletes make it a game and compete with themselves—trying to run faster or be more accurate than the day before. Others take a more creative angle. Valarie Allman, a 2021 Olympic gold medalist, dreamed of being a dancer when she was in high school, even touring with dancers and choreographers from the TV show *So You Think You Can Dance*. But she also dabbled in track and field, never quite finding an event that suited her until she discovered the discus. Throwing the discus requires a rapid one-and-a-half-turn

In-Season and Off-Season Workouts

Superstars train all year around, but the kinds of workouts they do differ from the off-season to in-season training. Many athletes ease up on their workouts a little during the season so they have more energy for actual competitions. But then in the off-season, they can focus more on building muscle and endurance. Off-season training might also include work on parts of their game that need extra attention that the rigors of a busy schedule cannot accommodate. Toronto Raptors player Terrence Ross told Basketball Insiders before the start of the 2021–2022 NBA season that he used the off-season to work on improving his game in every way possible. "I've been putting a lot of focus on getting stronger too; that was the main goal for me this offseason. I want to continue to get stronger and be able to absorb contact better when I'm driving. I've been shooting a lot of mid-range shots, too." Of course, many superstars use the off-season to rest their tired bodies and spend time with their families since the regular season can make that challenging. But they cannot rest too much, because the next season is always right around the corner.

Quoted in Alex Kennedy, "NBA Players Discuss Offseason Improvement," Basketball Insiders, October 15, 2021. www.basketballinsiders.com.

rotation in a small circle, followed by the release of the discus and the extension of the throwing arm before bouncing or hopping to a stop. Allman found herself drawn to the event because it reminded her of dancing onstage. "I think it's a second-and-a-half dance that you do hundreds of times and it's really repetitive, but gosh-darn, I so think it's a dance," she told the *Washington Post* after winning her medal in Tokyo. "It's poetry. It's balance. It's grace. It's power."[17]

> "I can give her sets to do by herself or have her come in on her own for extra work and she doesn't bat an eye."[18]
>
> —Yuri Suguiyama, Olympic champion Katie Ledecky's swim coach

For Olympic gold medal–winning swimmer Katie Ledecky, skills training means swimming hundreds of laps in the pool most days of the week. A typical day for Ledecky starts with more than 6,000 meters, or about 130 laps in an Olympic-sized, 50-meter pool. Later in the day, she will add another 7,000 to 8,000 meters to her daily count. This is on top of the strength training, stretching, and other exercises she does all year round. "I can give her sets to do by herself or have her come in on her own for extra work and she doesn't bat an eye,"[18] her coach Yuri Suguiyama told *Swimming World* magazine.

Like Ledecky, many superstars do not think twice about putting in extra effort to maintain or improve their skills because they have always approached their sport that way. There are countless stories of top athletes practicing specific skills over and over until they mastered them. American soccer superstar Christian Pulisic's mom, Kelley, recalled young Christian endlessly practicing kicks with his left foot so that he would not rely so much on his dominant right foot. In his Hershey, Pennsylvania, backyard, where his soccer coach father had set up a goal, Christian did everything with his left foot that he did with his right. "He said, 'Okay, I'm going to do 50 with my right leg, now I'm going to do 50 with my left leg. He would just get so mad if he couldn't get it," Pulisic's mother recalled. "He just would work on it: left foot, left foot, left foot hitting the upper corner."[19] Today one of Pulisic's strengths is his ability to switch directions instantly, leading with either foot to get past the defense.

Pursuit of Perfection

While it is true that many young athletes grow up with natural abilities that set them apart from their peers, the true superstars do not stop there. They have dreams of glory and championships. Sometimes those dreams are enough to get them out of bed early every morning to practice or to skip a high school party because they have to rest before a big competition. For some there is a coach or parent encouraging them to keep reaching and striving to maximize their potential. And for most young athletes, there is a love of the game that keeps bringing them out to practice season after season. But on top of that, there is a burning desire to be the best athletes they can be. Before he became the number one pick in the 2021 NFL draft, Clemson University quarterback Trevor Lawrence wanted to make sure no one doubted his work ethic and desire to become a champion. In a single tweet, Lawrence summed up how most superstars approach their sports: "I am driven to be the best I can be, and to maximize my potential. And to WIN."[20]

CHAPTER TWO

Mental Toughness

New York Yankees Hall of Fame catcher Yogi Berra once said, "Baseball is 90 percent mental. The other half is physical."[21] Berra was known for his humorous, if somewhat head-scratching, assessments of sports and life. Setting aside his lopsided math, Berra was onto something with his explanation that success in sports relies largely on an athlete's mind. The ability to focus, remain confident, and rapidly learn and apply new information is a trait shared by most sports superstars.

Having those skills is one thing. Being able to summon them during a critical moment in a game or competition is what separates the superstars from the rest of their athletic peers—and in many cases, from nonathletes, too. A British study comparing the memory tasks and decision-making skills of champion athletes and nonathletes found that superstars tend to respond faster and more accurately, especially under pressure. Lead researcher Vincent Walsh, a professor at University College London's Institute of Cognitive Neuroscience, told the *Daily Mail* newspaper:

> These elite athletes perform tasks that many of us could never comprehend, but what is fascinating is their mindset when tackling such challenges. When some decisions can be the difference between success and failure, it is perhaps unsurprising that the study showed that athletes were consistently several seconds faster

when performing their tasks. A few seconds or a few percent may not sound like much, but this is a long time in sport, and is the difference between winning and losing.[22]

Being able to process constantly changing information and situations quickly is essential in many sports. NFL quarterback Peyton Manning was always considered a great student of the game, studying film of his opponents for hours on end and rapidly thinking through all the scenarios that could occur on every play. Manning often left the huddle and walked up to the line of scrimmage, scanned the defense's formation, and at the last second changed the play, yelling out new signals before taking the snap

Superstar athletes often need to process constantly changing information and situations. Here, Denver Broncos head coach John Fox is pictured having a discussion with quarterback Peyton Manning during a 2013 game in Denver, Colorado.

and completing a pass for a first down. His former coach John Fox told *USA Today* that Manning may not have had the strongest arm, but he could think through any situation as well as or better than anyone else playing the position. "So much of it is decision-making and playing fast, doing things quickly and accurately," Fox said. "And that's what sets him apart."[23]

Confidence and Focus

Along with being able to make rapid-fire decisions under pressure, there may be no more common thread among all superstar athletes than confidence. It is not an unrealistic belief that they will be successful every time but rather a mindset that allows great athletes to compete at the highest levels without worrying about losing or coming up short. Most superstars have such trust in their abilities that they expect greatness and do not spend a lot of energy second-guessing themselves. All-Star NBA guard Victor Oladipo told the *Indianapolis Star* after hitting a game-winning shot at the buzzer, that he remains confident throughout a game, even if he has struggled early on. "I believe it's going in every time, no matter what I did the first three quarters. When it's winning time, it's a whole new game,"[24] he said.

Of course, it is normal to have doubts and concerns about unwanted outcomes. Many athletes and professional sports teams work with sports psychologists to help them maintain or restore their confidence during a slump or when recovering from an injury. Because in the end, having confidence can make the difference between winning and losing. "Years of sport psychology research tells us that confidence is the key differentiating psychological factor between successful and unsuccessful performance in a variety of sporting settings,"[25] says British sports psychologist Elliott Newell.

> "Years of sport psychology research tells us that confidence is the key differentiating psychological factor between successful and unsuccessful performance in a variety of sporting settings."[25]
>
> —Elliott Newell, sports psychologist

Prioritizing Mental Health

Growing up in Minnesota, cross-country skier Jessie Diggins became so consumed with trying to be perfect as a teenager that she developed a severe eating disorder. Through the help of a recovery program called the Emily Program, Diggins overcame her battle with bulimia and went on to win three Olympic medals. Rather than hide her struggles, Diggins has shared her story countless times in interviews, speaking engagements, and her memoir. "I want people to know that you don't have to be perfect. I'm definitely not," she says. "I have a lot of things that I'm working on, but I think my biggest strength is that I do ask for help now." Only in recent years has the issue of mental health become a subject that athletes willingly discuss. Like Diggins, fellow Olympians Michael Phelps and gymnast Suni Lee have also spoken out about their struggles with depression and anxiety, letting the world know that success in sports does not make someone immune to such problems. By sharing their stories, these superstars hope to inspire others grappling with personal challenges. "I know I'm not alone," Phelps said during the 2021 Olympics. "And I understand that for me it's OK to not be OK."

Quoted in Lisa Antonucci, "Jessie Diggins' Legacy Extends Far Beyond Her Historic Olympic Gold," NBC Sports, February 5, 2022. https://onherturf.nbcsports.com.

Quoted in Olympics, "Michael Phelps: 'Don't Be Afraid to Dream as Big as You Possibly Can,'" October 5, 2021 https://olympics.com.

Part of what boosts athletes' confidence is the preparation they put in to get ready to perform and the ability to focus on their goals and game plans while ignoring distractions like fans, the media, and other concerns. During his record-breaking senior season at Louisiana State University, quarterback Joe Burrow accidentally broke his cell phone. When his parents offered to get him a new one, he declined, telling them he had a football game to play that week and did not need the distraction of social media or texts. That is just one example of how Burrow's ability to focus helped him lead the Tigers to a national championship. Just before Burrow was drafted by the Cincinnati Bengals to begin his NFL career, his college coach, Ed Orgeron, told the media, "Joe is probably the most focused player I've been around. We gave him the team. . . . I think his work ethic and his smarts is going to make him a great player."[26]

Like Burrow, who led the Bengals to the Super Bowl in 2022, other superstars know the key to being focused in sports means taking care of your responsibilities without paying attention to what your competition is up to or what critics say. Superstars know that if they just play their game, run their race, or do whatever else is required in their sport, they have the best chance of being successful. US track star Sydney McLaughlin broke a world record in the 400-meter hurdles when she won the gold medal in the 2021 Summer Olympics in Tokyo. She credited her ability to tune out what the other runners were doing and everything else going on around her in order to run the race of her life. Afterward, she told *Time* magazine:

> "The biggest lesson the sport has ever taught me, at this moment in time, is really to just focus on your lane. Everybody's journey in the sport looks different."[27]
>
> —Sydney McLaughlin, US Olympic champion hurdler

> The biggest lesson the sport has ever taught me, at this moment in time, is really to just focus on your lane. Everybody's journey in the sport looks different. Nothing is ever guaranteed from year to year. So, taking the opportunities that you have in front of you and not looking around at what everyone else is doing. It's so much easier said than done. But truly for me, focusing on my lane and my 10 hurdles, whatever that looks like in whatever capacity, truly does make the difference instead of running somebody else's race.[27]

Staying Composed

Because the nature of competition is unpredictable, most truly successful athletes know how to keep their composure when things are not going well or when they are about to compete for a championship. Many athletes say the keys to remaining calm involve things like visualizing various outcomes and relying on routines that have been established for years.

Allyson Felix, an American sprinter who has won eleven Olympic medals and is the most decorated American track-and-field athlete in history, relies on visualization to tamp down the pressure of an Olympic race or any other big challenge in her life. She says:

> Every four years I have this opportunity—for only about 21 seconds—to get it right. It can be a really big moment, so it's just really about quieting my mind, closing my eyes, and really going through the motions of what the perfect race looks like. I find it's helpful for me to run through what that looks like before I go into a very stressful situation.[28]

Tennis legend Serena Williams plays at Wimbledon in 2021. Williams once explained to an interviewer that keeping one's composure is important for an athlete, because it allows them to make good decisions in the heat of the moment.

Staying cool under pressure also comes from learning to rely on experience and skills. Athletes who have faced similar situations many times can instinctively react rather than think too much and let the pressure of the moment take over. Tennis star Serena Williams, who has won more Grand Slam singles titles than anyone else in the Open Era (which began in 1968), explained to an interviewer that staying composed is the key to making good decisions in the heat of the moment. This applies to all of life's challenges, not just those in sports. Williams says:

> When something comes up, I also think of 20 different ways to solve it . . . and I think it's because on the tennis court, when you go for a shot, you have 0.2 seconds to decide if you want to go to the left, the right, the middle or how you're going to counteract the shot if it's a difficult ball. I think that has trained my mind to make decisions quickly and make the best decision I can in the moment with all the pressure. You have to remain calm.[29]

Learning from Losses

Remaining calm and cool after a loss can be a challenge for anyone, including superstar athletes. Few of them have careers unblemished by mistakes or heartbreaking losses. In fact, many athletes and coaches say they remember the losses and the moments they came up short far more clearly than the wins. Part of that may be because pain and disappointment can often be stronger emotions than happiness. But top athletes also know that losing can provide valuable lessons.

Losses help them recognize things they need to improve upon and mistakes to avoid next time. Being able to come back from a tough loss to compete again even harder represents growth—not just as an athlete, but as a person. Williams admits that as much as she hates losing—she does not even like to say the word—she understands that without the losses along the way, she might not

> "As much as I hate it, some of my best growth has come from a loss."[30]
>
> —Serena Williams, US tennis champion

have become a champion. "As much as I hate it, some of my best growth has come from a loss," she shares. "And for me to actually get to the next level, like, I would've never won that Grand Slam or that tournament had I not lost to that person on that day, no matter how much it hurt."[30]

Losing a game or making mistakes can only occur when someone is making an effort. The superstars who push themselves do so knowing that losing is a possibility, but so is winning. In a famous commercial for Nike, NBA legend Michael Jordan says, "I've missed more than 9,000 shots in my career. I've lost almost 300 games. Twenty-six times I've been trusted to take the game-winning shot and missed. I've failed over and over and over again in my life. And that is why I succeed."[31]

Resilience

Losing a big game or a meet or other contest is not the only type of setback superstars must overcome. They often have to battle injuries, illness, or setbacks like getting benched because of poor play or failing to make a team's roster despite months or years of training. And they have to have the mental toughness to put in the work to reach their athletic goals and not give up.

Major League Baseball player Trey Mancini was a rising young star with the Baltimore Orioles when he was diagnosed with colon cancer in 2020, just before his twenty-eighth birthday. Throughout his chemotherapy treatments, he wondered whether his weakened body would ever allow him to once again play the sport he loved. But he never gave up, and in 2021 he was back in an Orioles uniform, finishing second in the Home Run Derby at the All-Star Game and winning Comeback Player of the Year. Overcoming adversity not only confirms that superstars

> "I've failed over and over and over again in my life. And that is why I succeed."[31]
>
> —Michael Jordan, NBA Hall of Famer

can accomplish great things, it can also give them a perspective that keeps them grounded and appreciative of having a second chance. At the start of that amazing comeback season in 2021, Mancini said, "I'm very proud of where I am right now. Feeling like myself and feeling great is something I am very appreciative of and don't take for granted at all. I'm hoping to take a lot of that perspective into this year. I really think I'm going to appreciate—not that I didn't before—but I will *really* appreciate being able to play Major League Baseball every single day."[32]

For superstars who have been on top of the world and suffered major injuries or other setbacks, a long recovery can be especially challenging because they know an athlete's prime years are limited and they know what it took to reach the pinnacle the first time. Like Mancini, who quietly wondered whether he would ever get back to the major leagues, American skier Lindsey Vonn also had her doubts while recuperating from injuries that kept her

American skier Lindsey Vonn is pictured at the 2010 Winter Olympics in Vancouver. After winning a gold medal that year, Vonn struggled through injury, surgery, and rehabilitation, finally coming back to win another medal at the 2018 Olympics.

off the slopes for almost two years. In 2010 Vonn had become the first American woman to win an Olympic downhill gold medal, but injuries in 2013 and 2014 put her future skiing career in jeopardy. Still, she underwent knee surgery and embarked on a grueling rehabilitation program and training regimen to get ready for the 2014–2015 World Cup season. She performed well for the next couple of years, only to break her arm at the end of 2016 during a training run.

By the time the 2018 Winter Olympics in South Korea arrived, Vonn was ready to see whether another medal was possible. And in the downhill, her specialty, Vonn won the bronze medal. Shortly afterward, she broke down in tears, recalling all the pain and struggle she had been through just to get back on the medal stand. "It's so rewarding," she said. "Of course I would have liked a gold medal, but this is amazing and I am so proud. I gave it my best shot. I worked my butt off."[33]

Calming Meditation

LeBron James may be best known for his on-court skills that have made him one of the greatest basketball players in history. And while his training and fitness routines have allowed him to play for nearly twenty years and win multiple MVP Awards and NBA championships, he also credits meditation for his success. James meditates several times a day to help stay calm and focused during games and away from the arena when dealing with family, the media, his business endeavors, and everyday life. He says, "Meditating helps a lot for me personally with taking a lot of deep breaths, closing my eyes and just centering myself and listening to my inner self." James has even been known to close his eyes and meditate briefly when he is on the bench in the middle of a game. Many other superstars, including NFL quarterback Russell Wilson and tennis star Novak Djokovic, use meditation to relax and to refocus their thoughts, blocking out the distractions and unhelpful or negative thoughts that might affect their performance.

Quoted in 3cbPerformance, "Explained: Why LeBron James Meditates During Games," Silver Screen and Roll, March 1, 2022. www.silverscreenandroll.com.

Becoming Mentally Tough

Having the mental toughness to recover from injury, block out distractions, and thrive under pressure may seem like a natural characteristic of superstar athletes. Certainly, plenty of superstars grow up with a drive to succeed that surprises even their parents. Others survive a difficult childhood that instills a toughness that they channel into their sport.

But mental toughness is also a skill that can be learned. Sometimes kids learn toughness and a strong work ethic by watching their parents. Baseball slugger Bryce Harper's dad was an ironworker who put in long days on construction sites before coming home to play catch or pitch batting practice to his future major leaguer. Of his dad and his own determination to improve his strength and skills, Harper says, "Watching my pops get up every single morning, going into work, working hard — I think that really made me want to work that hard, wanted to make me get up early and go for a run or get a lift in or get some extra hitting in and really try to better myself everyday."[34]

Lessons in mental toughness can come from anywhere—even from fans. Years before he faced his own battle with cancer, Trey Mancini became close to Mo Gaba, a young Orioles fan with cancer. During the All-Star break in 2018, when a lot of players who do not make the All-Star game take off for mini-vacations, Mancini chose to spend a day with Mo and his mother Sonsy. "I hung out with him and his mom all day and it was just one of the best days I've ever had honestly," Mancini said in a 2019 interview. "It put some things in perspective. If somebody can stay that positive, then you know your problems in life aren't too tough."[35]

CHAPTER THREE

Superstar Support

When Olympic figure skating gold medalist Nathan Chen was three years old, his mother placed him in her Prius and drove to a nearby ice rink to introduce her boy to a sport that would take him around the world and to the pinnacle of athletic success. And in the days following his gold medal–winning performance in the 2022 Winter Olympics, Chen recalled many more hours in that Prius traveling to and from practices and competitions with his number one fan. "Absolutely none of this would be at all remotely possible without her support," he told *Today*. "Since day one, 3 years old, I stepped on the ice, and she's been by my side ever since."[36]

On Instagram, taking a post-Olympic drive in the family car with his mom to see his sisters, Chen further acknowledged the selfless role she played in driving from their home in Utah to California for meets and coaching opportunities: "It made me emotional to think of how tirelessly she supported me in my skating career, not once complaining that the drive was too long or too hard. Without her support, I never would have made it to where I am now."[37]

While not all superstar athletes have a parent who made their sports dreams come true, many of them do. Or they have a coach who believed in them and helped them reach their potential. Or maybe it was a teacher or a grandparent or someone else in their lives who fueled that dream when it really was just that: a dream to be a champion. On the way to superstardom, and even after they have arrived, superstars rely on teammates, trainers, coaches, psychologists, and others who contribute in some way to their success. As with anyone who is successful in business, politics, the arts, or any other field, superstar athletes do not reach the top all on their own, and they definitely do not stay there without a lot of support and guidance from others.

> "Without [my mother's] support, I never would have made it to where I am now."[37]
>
> —Nathan Chen, Olympic ice-skating champion

Support from the Start

From T-ball fields to high school gyms and all the sporting venues in between, an athlete's family members and friends can often be found cheering for victories and consoling their bud-

American figure skater Nathan Chen is pictured at the 2022 Winter Olympics in Beijing, where he won a gold medal. Chen said that his success would not have been possible without the support of his mother.

ding superstars who do not finish on top. And when athletes ascend to the top and have their games televised, TV cameras often capture proud parents, spouses, children, and other loved ones reacting to all the ups and downs of competition. The smiles and tears all tell stories of how loved ones support the athlete's journey—the early-morning practices, the long road trips, the injuries and recoveries, the wins, the losses, and the marking of time with one sports season rolling into the next.

And for many superstars, the big moments are not the same without their friends' and family's support in the stands. When Cincinnati Bengals defensive back Tre Flowers played in the Super Bowl in 2022, he made sure his mother, Crystal, and father, Rodney, were there. Crystal, who has been cheering for her son since he was a little boy, would not have had it any other way. She says, "I still think I'm at one of his little pee wee games and I'm just in the stands. I mean, I get choked up about it. I just see him and he said, 'Mom you got to be here. I need you here when we win.' He's just so humble and puts us first."[38]

But sometimes circumstances do not allow parents to be there in person. So when the Tokyo Summer Olympics in 2021 and Beijing Winter Olympics in 2022 were held without the athletes' friends and families able to attend because of COVID-19 safety protocols, NBC Sports arranged for the athletes performing in Asia to connect with their loved ones back in the United States through video feeds from watch parties, usually in the homes of the athletes' parents. The video chats usually involved lots of smiles and tears, with choked-up athletes confessing how much they missed their families and how much it helped them perform knowing their loved ones were watching, even if it was from halfway around the world. When US swimmer Caeleb Dressel won the 100-meter freestyle in Tokyo, he told an NBC reporter how hard the past year had been with COVID-19-related limits on training, travel, and the presence of

Some superstar athletes began their careers with parents, grandparents, and other relatives as their only fans and coaches. Football quarterback Patrick Mahomes is pictured here in 2013 with his father, Pat; younger brother, Jackson; and mother, Randi.

family at most competitions. But everything seemed okay when a nearby TV monitor showed his new wife, Meghan, his parents, and more than a dozen other friends and relatives crowded in front of the TV cheering for him. Dressel broke down in joyful tears, as did Meghan—and plenty of TV viewers at home. "That was the first time I got to talk to them," Dressel said moments later. "That was really special."[39]

Parents, grandparents, and other relatives are often the first fans and coaches a young athlete has. They are the ones volunteering to play catch in the backyard, time races at swim meets, sew ice-skating costumes, have snacks ready after practice, and put countless miles on the family car to support their child's passion for sports. And many parents also make even greater sacrifices. When NBA star Kevin Durant won the MVP Award in 2014, he gave a legendary acceptance speech, giving all the credit for his success to his mother, who, as a single mom, kept Kevin and his sister and brothers safe and provided for them under very difficult circumstances in Washington, DC. Durant addressed his mother during his speech:

> You wake me up in the middle of the night in the summer times, making me run up a hill, making me do pushups, screaming at me from the sidelines of my games at 8 or 9 years old. We wasn't supposed to be here. You made us believe. You kept us off the street. You put clothes on our backs, food on the table. When you didn't eat, you made sure we ate. You went to sleep hungry. You sacrificed for us. You the real MVP.[40]

It Takes Teamwork

The MVPs certainly get most of the attention from fans and the media, but they are often quick to acknowledge not just the parents who were there at the start but also their teammates who work just as hard throughout the seasons. When Edmonton Oilers hockey sensation Connor McDavid scored one hundred points in the 2016–2017 season and won the Art Ross Trophy as the National Hockey League's (NHL) leading scorer, he was quick to share the credit. "I wouldn't be here without my teammates,"[41] he told reporters shortly after learning he had won the coveted prize.

When superstars in team sports win championships, they do so playing alongside other great athletes. Stephen Curry needed fellow guard Klay Thompson to win NBA titles. US women's soccer star Megan Rapinoe won a World Cup and Olympic gold medal buoyed by the outstanding play of teammate Alex Morgan. In track and field, the best relay teams need all four runners to perform at their best, not just the star of the team.

When a superstar is having an off night, teammates can often step up

> "I wouldn't be here without my teammates."[41]
> —Connor McDavid, NHL scoring leader

Nutritionists Craft Winning Recipes

Superstar athletes certainly stay in shape by exercising and playing their sport, but that is not the only key to fitness. Athletes have to eat right, too, and that often means working with a nutritionist not only to plan healthy meals but also to make sure they are getting the right mix of protein, carbohydrates, vitamins, and other nutrients necessary for optimal health and performance. WNBA basketball star Sue Bird turned to a nutritionist in her thirties when she realized she did not have the energy she once did and did not seem to recover from tough workouts quite as readily as she did when she was younger. "I met with a nutritionist, who had me jot down what I was eating for the whole month," Bird told *Women's Health* magazine. "Then, he built a plan for me, all centered around having energy, fueling for workouts, and recovering from workouts." Sports nutritionists and dietitians can be essential parts of an athlete's support team. They work not only with young athletes to help them learn how to eat properly but also with older athletes to extend their careers by teaching them how to eat wisely and in some cases maintain a healthy weight.

Quoted in Jennifer Nied, "Olympic Basketball Star Sue Bird, 40, Changed Her Diet 6 Years Ago and Never Looked Back," *Women's Health*, July 23, 2021. www.womenshealthmag.com.

---

to get a win despite their star playing poorly. And when a superstar athlete hits an especially rough patch, teammates can provide some crucial emotional support. Going into the 2022 Winter Olympics, US skier Mikaela Shiffrin was expected to win medals in multiple events. She was essentially the face of the US team, but mishaps and falls kept her off the medals stand entirely. Devastated and disappointed, Shiffrin said toward the end of the games, "My teammates are what carried me through this Olympics."[42]

Just as superstars commonly praise their teammates, the athletes who play alongside the stars are often equally effusive about the individuals who win the awards and accolades. Many of the all-time greats can attract good players to their teams, not just because of their talent but also because superstars set

> Superstar athletes frequently admit that their success would not be possible without the efforts of their teammates. Here, US soccer star Megan Rapinoe (right) celebrates with teammate Alex Morgan at the 2019 FIFA Women's World Cup in Reims, France.

a tone for a team and understand the value of working together toward a common goal. NFL running back LeSean McCoy said of his superstar quarterback Tom Brady, "He's the best teammate, competitor, and leader I've ever seen in my life. He's the only player I've ever been around, quarterback, coach, that what he says, you believe it."[43]

Getting Great Coaching

As much as superstars rely on talented and supportive teammates, they also depend on coaches, who usually serve many roles in the life of an athlete. They may be parental figures, inspirational leaders, and teachers. And the people who coach great players know that another part of their job is to help the superstars know how to bring out the best in their teammates, especially those who come off the bench in certain situations. These athletes include relief pitchers in baseball and defensive specialists in basketball, and are known as role players, without whom many superstars would never reach their own potential and win a championship. The successful coaches know how to create a team out of superstars and role players and lead them all to a championship.

Dave "Doc" Roberts was hired to manage the Los Angeles Dodgers in 2016 after the team seemed to underperform year after year. The Dodgers had a mix of superstar pitchers, such as Clayton Kershaw and Kenley Jansen, as well as other rising stars like Corey Seager and Joc Pederson. Roberts found a way to allow his superstars to shine and made sure everybody on the team felt just as valuable. After the Dodgers lost a heartbreaking World Series in 2018—and before returning to claim the title in 2020—Jansen said of his manager, "What he built around here in the clubhouse, it wasn't like this before he came here. This is more of a team now with everyone united and how everyone is. Doc kind of built this, it's one team. It's not about one player, it's one team. We buy into that and try to win a championship."[44]

As much as head coaches and managers are responsible for creating a winning atmosphere and a winning game plan, other types of coaches help athletes become superstars through instruction. Teams in all sports have strength coaches whose job is to keep players strong, flexible, fit, and able to endure the grind of a season. Teams also have offensive and defensive specialists. And in some sports, there are coaches for specific positions. Hall of Fame quarterback John Elway had an amazing career, but it was not until a new quarterbacks coach was hired by the Denver

Broncos that Elway became a Super Bowl–winning quarterback—twice—later in his career. Elway told ESPN:

> When you create that trust in that quarterbacks coach, there's nothing more important than that for the quarterback to be successful. As QB, your relationship with your QB coach, but also your coordinator, is important—to know he's going to put you in the best situations to be successful and take advantage of your strengths and try to stay away from your weaknesses. For a QB, that's vital.[45]

In individual sports, athletes rely heavily on their coaches, because there are no teammates around to turn to for guidance or support. Practices for golfers, tennis players, ice skaters, gymnasts, and others are often one-on-one sessions with the athlete

Agents Guide Superstars' Careers

Sports agents may be most known for negotiating big contracts for their superstar clients, but many agents do much more than that. Agents of young athletes often serve as advisers, helping them buy their first house or make other important decisions. Good agents help athletes plan their careers and work to put their clients in the best position for success. That might mean advising a player to take less money to go with a team that will surround a superstar with great teammates and is good enough to win a championship. Sometimes an agent will make sure an athlete gets a second opinion before having surgery or another procedure recommended by the team. Agents often help their clients arrange for trainers, nutritionists, psychologists, and others to help maximize an athlete's potential. And sometimes an agent will have to help a client deal with problems, such as family squabbles, money concerns, a lack of playing time, poor media coverage, or other challenges. "Ultimately, good agents take care of a wide variety of issues and headaches that, individually or together, distract players from what they are being paid to do," longtime sportswriter Mike Florio wrote on his blog, *ProFootballTalk*.

Mike Florio, "Good Agents Do a Lot More than Negotiate Contracts," *ProFootballTalk* (blog), NBC Sports, July 23, 2015. https://profootballtalk.nbcsports.com.

and the coach. The relationship is often like a partnership. During practices and competitions, the coach calls the shots. But the rest of the time, the athlete is in charge, because the coach works for and is paid by the athlete. As a result, some superstar athletes have multiple coaches throughout their careers. Others enjoy success with a longtime coach at their side.

Bob Bowman was swimmer Michael Phelps's coach from the time Phelps was eleven years old through the Olympic champion's retirement in 2016. In many ways Bowman was a father figure to Phelps, whose parents divorced when he was young. Phelps even named his son Boomer Robert Phelps after his longtime coach, mentor, and friend. "Bob knows Michael like the back of his hand," Phelps's mother, Debbie said. "Michael knows Bob's going to get him where he needs to be, not only in the pool, but life."[46]

> "Average players want to be left alone. Good players want to be coached. Great players want to be told the truth."[47]
>
> —Glenn "Doc" Rivers, NBA head coach

As great as some athletes are, they can all benefit by learning from excellent coaches. That means superstars may have to set aside their egos and accept criticism from their coaches and be willing to learn new skills or new ways of approaching their sport. And the best players know this. NBA coach and former player Glenn "Doc" Rivers once said, "Average players want to be left alone. Good players want to be coached. Great players want to be told the truth."[47]

Sports Trainers Keep Superstars in Shape

On the sidelines in most sports, usually not far from the coaches, are the trainers who tend to injuries and make sure athletes are physically ready to perform at their best before and during competitions. They also help athletes recover after a competition or workout. And one of the biggest and most important responsibilities for a sports trainer is to help an athlete recover from a major injury.

When Devon Travis was playing second base for the Toronto Blue Jays, he had a few shoulder and knee injuries that threatened his career. But he worked closely with Blues Jays head athletic trainer Nikki Huffman—only the second woman to hold that job in any of North America's four major team sports—and after every injury he was back on the field playing as well as ever. Travis told a reporter with the Sportsnet TV channel:

> She doesn't want the credit for what she brings to this organization and what she's done but I want her to be recognized because she's great. She's the same person every day. She shows up. She does everything for everyone in this clubhouse. There's never a panic. "OK, you're feeling this? Let's try this. You didn't like that? Well, let's try this." That's her most special attribute. There isn't anything that is too big. If it's not working, we'll keep working, we'll keep trying until it does work. That's everything you look for in a trainer.[48]

Many superstar athletes have personal trainers to keep them in shape in the off-season, too. And if there is one thing superstars and their trainers know, it is that there are no shortcuts to success. The start of the next season may be months away, but the best athletes know they have to put in the time working out, training, studying, and maintaining their skills and fitness throughout the year. "Consistency is the king," says Idan Ravin, who has trained NBA stars Stephen Curry and LeBron James. "Becoming better and becoming great is not something that happens overnight. It's a lifelong pursuit."[49]

Whether it is family, teammates, coaches, trainers, or other people raising up superstar athletes and keeping them going, it is clear that no high performers get to the top by themselves. Likewise, no one stays there without a lot of support. The great athletes know this, and the humble ones readily admit it. After winning his third MVP Award in 2019, baseball slugger Mike Trout tweeted, "I am grateful to have coaches, teammates, family & a wife who continue to support me so I can play the game I love."[50]

CHAPTER FOUR

Seizing Opportunities

With six minutes left to play and his team down by four points in Super Bowl LVI, Los Angeles Rams quarterback Matthew Stafford calmly jogged onto the field knowing he had to move his team 79 yards (72.2 m) and into the opposite end zone to take the lead. In what is considered one of the greatest comeback drives in Super Bowl history, Stafford ignored the screaming fans and his team's struggles earlier in the game to connect on seven of eleven passes, including the game-winning touchdown pass to wide receiver Cooper Kupp with just over a minute to play. "You put the ball in your best players' hands when it matters the most, and that's what we did with Matthew," Rams coach Sean McVay said after the game. "And he delivered in a big way."[51]

The ability to deliver amazing performances when all eyes are on them is a trait shared by superstars in all sports. They do not shy away from the big moments. In fact, the superstars often perform at their best when everything is on the line. They seem to thrive under pressure. They want the spotlight and the responsibility for winning or losing the game. Rising NBA star Cade Cunningham of the Detroit Pistons told reporters after a win over the New York Knicks, "Any time the game is close or in crunch time I kind of feel like a magnet from my hands to the ball. I want the ball in my hands. My teammates trust me."[52]

When Their Number Is Called

While some superstars seem to have been in the spotlight since a young age—LeBron James was on the cover of *Sports Illustrated* when he was still in high school, and Serena Williams won her first US Open when she was just eighteen—others have taken a longer and more circuitous path to stardom. But at every step, those future superstars had to be ready to perform in case it was their one big chance. They kept in shape, did what coaches and trainers advised them to do, and did not say no to an opportunity, even if it was not exactly what they wanted or expected at that moment.

> "Any time the game is close or in crunch time I kind of feel like a magnet from my hands to the ball. I want the ball in my hands."[52]
>
> —Cade Cunningham, NBA star

Few all-time greats took a more unusual path to the top than NFL Hall of Fame quarterback Kurt Warner. He attended the University of Northern Iowa but did not become the starting quarterback until his senior year. He went undrafted but managed to get a tryout with the Green Bay Packers. He was released before start of the 1994 season, and with no other football prospects in sight, he took a job stocking shelves at the Hy-Vee grocery store in Cedar Rapids, Iowa, making $5.50 an hour. The next year Warner played in the indoor Arena Football League and was later signed by the Rams, who promptly sent him to Amsterdam to play in NFL Europe—a sort of minor leagues for the NFL.

Warner eventually made the Rams' team in St. Louis, but he was the third-string quarterback and unlikely ever to get any playing time. However, when the second-string quarterback was traded and the starter was injured before the season, the Rams made Warner starter in 1999. All he did after that was have one of the greatest statistical seasons in NFL history and become Super Bowl

Superstar athletes have the ability to deliver amazing performances when all eyes are on them, as Los Angeles Rams quarterback Matthew Stafford (9) did when he threw this touchdown pass to wide receiver Cooper Kupp during the 2022 Super Bowl.

MVP when the Rams knocked off the Tennessee Titans in Super Bowl XXXIV. Soon after being voted into the NFL Hall of Fame in 2017, Warner told a reporter that all the unusual stops and detours of his football career allowed him to understand the importance of always being prepared and appreciative for every opportunity that comes along. He said, "Looking back, I'm grateful my career took the path that it did. The great thing is now I know the end of the story and I'm so grateful that it did play out this way."[53]

Though not every athlete had such a winding road to stardom, plenty of them did. And the ones who made the most of their opportunities and were ready to go when a coach or other decision maker was watching them closely were the ones who reached the top. Sometimes it can take many tries to get the chance to shine, which means superstars cannot quit or get discouraged. Like Warner, a lot of NFL stars bounced back

Why Some Athletes Thrive Under Pressure

Everybody faces stressful situations at times, but for athletes, dealing with high-pressure circumstances is literally an everyday part of the job. Sports psychologists say that athletes respond to stress in one of two ways. They can enter a challenge state, which means they channel the stress response in a positive way that improves their performance. Or they can enter a threat state, which negatively affects their performance. Regardless of which state a person goes into, parts of the human stress response are the same: the heart rate increases and muscles tense. But in the challenge state, blood vessels relax and allow for robust blood flow to the brain to enhance focus and decision-making. In the threat state, blood vessels narrow, reducing circulation to the brain and making it harder to concentrate and make the best decisions. The threat state can also lead people to doubt their abilities and add pressure to the situation. "The key difference between those who get the gold medal and those who don't is between the ears," says sports psychologist Martin Turner, who adds that with training a person can learn to view stressful situations as opportunities to succeed rather than conditions likely to end in failure.

Quoted in Amy Morin, "Why Successful People Don't Crumble Under Pressure," *Forbes*, August 7, 2014. www.forbes.com.

from getting cut. That includes wide receiver Wes Welker, who helped the New England Patriots win two Super Bowls after being cut by two different teams, and James Harrison, who was released by four different teams in his first two years, only to get a chance with the Pittsburgh Steelers, with whom he won a Super Bowl and an NFL Defensive Player of the Year Award. "Sometimes I have to pinch myself," Welker said after his first season in New England. "It was good when I came to New England because I finally felt wanted. It was the first time in my life that had happened."[54]

When Championships Are on the Line

Winning a Super Bowl or any major championship is usually the ultimate goal for most athletes. And such accomplishments are often what sports fans and members of the media tend to use when labeling an athlete a true superstar. Though there are plenty of sports legends who never won the ultimate prize in their sport, most athletes identified as superstars have a championship on their résumé. And more than that, these superstars often performed their best when it counted the most.

Longtime Yankees shortstop Derek Jeter epitomized the superstar who shone brightest in his sport's biggest games. In leading the Yankees to five World Series titles, Jeter set postseason records for hits, runs scored, and other categories while batting an impressive .321. During the regular season, Jeter was a consistent hitter and a decent shortstop, but when the playoffs arrived, he made so many big plays that he earned the nickname Captain Clutch.

Jeter famously smashed the very first pitch of the 2000 World Series against the New York Mets over the left field fence to set the stage for a dominating performance for his team and for Jeter himself, who hit a remarkable .409 and was named World Series MVP. Jeter's teammate Paul O'Neill describes the shortstop's ability to rise to the occasion in the playoffs this way: "The amazing thing about Derek was that he was never nervous. I mean lots of guys pretend they've got it under control, especially during the playoffs. Some guys are pretty good at acting that way. But with Derek, I always believed it was genuine. Nothing got to him, no matter what the situation."[55]

For Jeter and others who raise their game in the most important situations, the pressure is not a hindrance. In fact, such superstars want the attention and the responsibility of delivering when a championship is at stake. They crave those opportunities, while some athletes find the pressure to be too much to bear. Snowboarder Chloe Kim is one of those athletes

> "I like the pressure."[56]
>
> —Chloe Kim, Olympic snowboarding gold medalist

who seem especially relaxed and ready for anything when the pressure is the greatest. Just before her last run at the 2018 X Games, when she needed a near-perfect performance to win her fourth championship, she turned to her coach and said, "I like this. I like the pressure."[56] She then seemed to effortlessly put together a medal-winning run—evidence that the pressure only seemed to bring out her best.

One way superstar athletes are able to perform in the postseason like they do in the regular season is by treating every competition the same way. Stephen Curry goes through the same routine during the playoffs as he does during a typical week in the middle of the season. Like a lot of successful athletes, Curry will often eat the same food before a competition and warm up the same way. Breaking from the usual routine could become a distraction. Curry said in a *Men's Health* article:

> I don't know what I'll feel when I walk in the arena. There's no preparing yourself for that. But, I'm going to have the same routine from the time I shoot around to the time I go home to the time I go to the game, and that should hopefully be able to calm myself down. And once the game starts, your preparation should take over and you'll be ready to go.[57]

The most successful athletes are also able to remind themselves about their preparation and what got them to the moment when an Olympic medal or other prize was at stake. Two-time US national fencing champion and Olympic medalist Tim Morehouse

> "Why shouldn't I be the guy who wins the gold?"[58]
>
> —Tim Morehouse, US national fencing champion

once went up against the second-ranked sabre fencer in the world. But rather than be intimidated, Morehouse thought about his two previous victories over other highly ranked fencers. "I just looked at my opponent and said, 'Why

Superstars Without Championships

Every sport has a long list of astonishing athletes who never claimed the ultimate prize. For example, NFL quarterback Dan Fouts set dozens of passing records and was inducted into the Football Hall of Fame but never won a Super Bowl. Michelle Kwan, one of the most accomplished and admired ice skaters in US history, won five world championships, but in two Olympics earned only silver and bronze medals. Rather than let those disappointments shape their post-athletic careers, Fouts, Kwan, and many other superstars who came up just short of their sports dreams found success and rewards in other careers. Fouts has had a long career as a sports broadcaster, while Kwan has pursued a life in international diplomacy. She worked for the US Department of State for several years and in 2022 was named US ambassador to Belize. So while some superstars never get to claim the championships they dreamed of as children, they can use their skills as dedicated, resilient, and hardworking leaders to become superstars in new fields. They are reminders that the qualities of superstardom do not just apply to athletics.

shouldn't I be the guy who wins the gold?' Just asking that question made me feel like I could beat anybody."[58]

Leadership

Plenty of superstar athletes like Harrison and Welker were not recognized for their potential right away. Having had to work a little harder to get their chance, they tend to understand the challenges facing teammates and others in their sport. So it is not surprising that superstars are often great leaders, too. Some are quiet leaders, who prefer to lead by example rather than give pep talks and be very vocal. It is said that the greatest players in team sports are those who help everyone around them perform better, whether by creating opportunities for them to show off their strengths or by offering constructive criticism that never comes across as mean or critical. That was former San Antonio Spurs player Tim Duncan, who led his team to five NBA titles and won more games with one team than anyone else. At Duncan's retirement ceremony, teammate Tony Parker said of the famously quiet Duncan, "He makes everyone around him better and that's the definition of a superstar."[59]

While Duncan had little use for awards and accolades, other superstars naturally give the pregame speeches and step into the spotlight, accepting blame for losses and sharing credit with teammates for the victories. A great example of a vocal leader who does everything she can to boost teammates and represent her sport in a positive way is Chicago Sky forward Candace Parker, a two-time WNBA champion and seven-time All-Star. Parker is like a coach on the floor, instructing younger players where to play on defense and when to make the extra pass on offense. She takes younger players under her wing and in postgame press conferences offers praise to her teammates and even to her opponents. Her younger teammate Kahleah Copper says Parker's leadership on the team and in the league is a positive for everybody and part of why Parker is such a superstar. Copper explains:

> "[My teammate Tim Duncan] makes everyone around him better and that's the definition of a superstar."[59]
>
> —Tony Parker, NBA star

> She's very unselfish, and it's going to do nothing but grow the game. It doesn't even directly benefit her. It's a major plus. It speaks to who she is off the court. She shows genuine love and wants to help. She could've just been selfish and to herself and had it be all about her, but it was never like that. She's always complimenting other players. We've been in press conferences, and she's talking about Sabrina (Ionescu)'s triple-double. She don't want to be the only player. She wants the game to grow. She's acknowledging younger players.[60]

Like Parker, plenty of other superstars see themselves as ambassadors of their sport. They recognize that with popularity comes a responsibility to the next generation of athletes. Few superstars have taken on that role as enthusiastically and successfully as skateboarder Tony Hawk. The San Diego native went from being an awkward little kid trying to learn tricks in an empty swimming pool to a successful professional skater to an entrepreneur and philanthropist whose name is almost synonymous with skateboarding. As his fame and skills increased, Hawk

Chicago Sky basketball player Candace Parker (facing camera) encourages teammates during a 2021 game. Parker is a strong leader, and often helps and praises her teammates.

launched a massively successful video game series (*Tony Hawk's Pro Skater*) and started releasing instructional videos and holding clinics to inspire kids and people of all ages and walks of life to try skateboarding. He created the nonprofit Tony Hawk Foundation, which was renamed the Skatepark Project, to build skate parks in underprivileged communities around the world.

The idea for the foundation sprang from a skate park opening Hawk attended in an affluent Chicago suburb, where he noticed that the park was poorly designed and not accessible to kids who had few other well-made and well-maintained recreational spaces around them. He told the *San Diego Union-Tribune*, "The idea for the foundation was that I wanted to connect those dots, and make sure the skaters were involved in the process, the planning, even the building. But more so, that the funding goes toward needy areas. I felt like these facilities need to be in places where kids are really challenged and really at risk."[61]

Giving Back

Superstar athletes frequently give back to their fans and communities—in ways big and small. After Hurricane Harvey caused massive flooding and damage throughout the Houston area in 2017, Houston Texans defensive end JJ Watt helped raise $37 million for rebuilding and relief efforts. Other sports stars volunteer at sports camps and visit children in hospitals.

World Wrestling Entertainment (WWE) superstar John Cena has been actively involved with the Make-A-Wish Foundation. This is a non-profit organization that fulfills the wishes of children with serious medical conditions. The organization often arranges for a special meeting with a superstar athlete or other celebrity.

Cena has made more than 650 wishes come true for young fans through Make-A-Wish—a record for the organization. He usually brings a championship belt for kids to try on, gives them memorabilia and merchandise, tells stories about his life and career, and offers words of inspiration. These visits take place in

Professional wrestler John Cena poses with some children at the lighting ceremony in support of the Make-A-Wish Foundation at the Empire State Building in New York City on December 20, 2018. As of 2018, Cena had helped to make more than 650 wishes come true.

children's homes, hospital rooms, and even at the arenas where Cena performs. "There is no more humbling experience than a child who could ask for anything in the world asking to meet me," Cena said on the occasion of his 500th wish visit. "I have faced some of the toughest superstars in WWE history and I've never encountered more bravery or toughness than I see in each wish kid that I meet."[62]

Superstars Are Human, Too

Superstar athletes certainly have an impressive array of qualities: amazing skills, dedication to their sport, toughness, resilience, split-second decision-making, leadership, and so on. But world-famous sports stars can have plenty of flaws, too. They can get impatient and discouraged. They can make bad decisions. Injuries and age can affect their abilities. Their feelings can be hurt when they are booed by fans or read negative comments about themselves online or in the press. In other words, superstars are human.

In 2021 Simone Biles had to withdraw from the team gymnastics competition in the Tokyo Olympics because a mental health issue could have put her at risk of injury while doing some of her ambitious routines. She was lauded for speaking out about anxiety and the struggles she had faced as the pressure of the Olympic Games neared. Afterward, more athletes came forward to share their personal stories of anxiety, depression, and the challenges of performing at a high level amid the kinds of worries and difficulties that everyone deals with every day.

That superstars deal with many of the same problems as the rest of the world does shows that in many ways they are more like the average person than they are different. Though it is easier said than done, recognizing the humanness of superstar athletes means that just about anyone can be a superstar if that person chooses the right sport and puts in the time and effort to excel. And if not in sports, people can become superstars in some other walk of life. There are superstar parents, grandparents, teachers, doctors, nurses, and artists, for example. Being great at anything is often just a matter of figuring out the path to success and sticking to that path, regardless of the obstacles or distractions that come along. The key is to keep the big goals in mind and not allow doubt to get in the way. As swimmer Michael Phelps wrote in his book *No Limits*, "It doesn't matter if you fall short; it is never a failure to go after your goals with everything you've got."[63]

SOURCE NOTES

Introduction: A Superstar in the Making

1. Quoted in Drew Shiller, "Steph Curry Reveals Moment He Knew 'Basketball Was Going to Be My Life," NBC Bay Area, October 30, 2018. www.nbcbayarea.com.
2. Quoted in Mark Medina, "'He's in Love with Getting Better': How Stephen Curry Has Maintained Peak Conditioning," NBA, June 13, 2022. www.nba.com.
3. Quoted in Brandon Hall, "Draymond Green on the Incredible Power of Self-Confidence for Athletes," Stack, May 30, 2019. www.stack.com.
4. Quoted in 247Sports, "Stephen Curry Quotes." https://247sports.com.

Chapter One: Maximizing Potential

5. Quoted in Alexis Farah, "Olympian Simone Biles Dishes on How She's Training, Eating, and Mentally Prepping Before Rio," *Women's Health*, July 29, 2016. www.womenshealthmag.com.
6. Quoted in Lydialyle Gibson, "A Fast Start," *Harvard Magazine*, July–August 2016. www.harvardmagazine.com.
7. Quoted in Ebenezer Samuel, "Patrick Mahomes Doesn't Take a Day Off," *Men's Health*, February, 8, 2021. www.menshealth.com.
8. Quoted in Samuel, "Patrick Mahomes Doesn't Take a Day Off."
9. Quoted in Diana Bocco, "10 Questions with Champion Snowboarder Lindsey Jacobellis," *The Clymb* (blog). https://blog.theclymb.com.
10. Quoted in Sauvik Banerjee, "Kyler Murray Opens Up on Why He Chose the Gridiron over the Diamond: 'Picking Football over Baseball Was One of the Hardest Decisions I've Ever Had to Make," EssentiallySports, April 22, 2022. www.essentiallysports.com.
11. Quoted in Elliott Almond, "Kick-Starting Their Careers: For Olajuwon, Ewing and Others, Athletics Began with Soccer," *Los Angeles Times*, May 22, 1994. www.latimes.com.
12. Quoted in Matt Foreman, "Interview: Travis Cooper," Catalyst Athletics, December 9, 2015. www.catalystathletics.com.
13. Quoted in Dan Pompei, "In Better Shape than Ever at Age 39: Here's How Tom Brady Does It," Bleacher Report, January 12, 2017. https://bleacherreport.com.
14. Quoted in Megan Falk, "Chloe Kim Reveals the Training Routine and Life Lessons That Helped Her Make Olympic History," *Shape*, February 16, 2022. www.shape.com.

15. Quoted in Falk, "Chloe Kim Reveals the Training Routine and Life Lessons That Helped Her Make Olympic History."
16. Quoted in Christa Sgobba, "My Bedtime Routine: Sue Bird on How Fiancée Megan Rapinoe Saved Her Skin," *SELF*, July 23, 2021. www.self.com.
17. Quoted in Roman Stubbs, "In the Driving Rain, a Former Dancer Wins Gold in the Discus Throw for Team USA," *Washington Post*, August 2, 2021. www.washingtonpost.com.
18. Quoted in *Swimming World*, "Training of Katie Ledecky: A Glance at Workouts That Led to First Olympic Title," July 5, 2021. www.swimmingworldmagazine.com.
19. Quoted in Oliver Franklin-Wallis, "America Finally Has a Global Soccer Star," *GQ*, January 19, 2021. www.gq.com.
20. Quoted in Timothy Rapp, "Trevor Lawrence Clarifies Remarks: 'I Love Football as Much or More than Anyone.'" Bleacher Report, April 17, 2021. https://bleacherreport.com.

Chapter Two: Mental Toughness

21. Quoted in Michael Chen, "Yogi Berra's Famous Quotes: 'Baseball Is 90 Percent Mental. The Other Half Is Physical," *Globe and Mail* (Toronto), September 23, 2015. www.theglobeandmail.com.
22. Quoted in Kate Pickles, "How Sports Stars Perform Better than Most Under Pressure: Athletes and Racing Drivers 'Think Faster and More Accurately When Stressed,'" *Daily Mail* (London), October 17, 2016. www.dailymail.co.uk.
23. Quoted in Lindsay H. Jones, "For Peyton Manning, a Remarkable Mind Always Was Critical to His Success," *USA Today*, March 7, 2016. www.usatoday.com.
24. Quoted in J. Michael, "Indiana Pacers Complete Best Road Trip of Season in Coming Back to Beat Dallas Mavericks," *Indianapolis Star*, March 8, 2020. www.indystar.com.
25. Elliott Newell, "Understanding Confidence in Sport," Believe Perform, 2022. https://believeperform.com.
26. Quoted in Mike Triplett, "LSU's Ed Orgeron Says Joe Burrow Willing to Face Adversity at the Next Level," ESPN, April 21, 2020. www.espn.com.au.
27. Quoted in Sean Gregory, "Sydney McLaughlin Is the 400-m Hurdles World Record Holder. But Her Journey Is Just Beginning," *Time*, August 3, 2021. https://time.com.
28. Quoted in Lauren Valenti, "Train like a Pro: How Olympic Track Star Allyson Felix Keeps Her Mind and Body Strong," *Vogue*, November 22, 2201. www.vogue.com.
29. Quoted in Lindsay Holmes, "Serena Williams Gets Real About Managing Anxiety," HuffPost, April 26, 2018. www.huffpost.com.
30. Quoted in Melissa Angell, "Serena Williams to Startup Founders: Admit Your Losses If You Want to Win," *Inc.*, February 4, 2022. www.inc.com.
31. Quoted in Eric Zorn, "Without Failure, Jordan Would Be False Idol," *Chicago Tribune*, May 19, 1997. www.chicagotribune.com.

32. Quoted in Joe Trezza, "Inside Mancini's Inspiring Return to Baseball," MLB.com, March 30, 2021. www.mlb.com.
33. Quoted in Stephanie Webber, "Lindsey Vonn Breaks Down in Tears After Winning Bronze at 2018 Olympics," *Us Weekly*, February 21, 2018. www.usmagazine.com.
34. Quoted in Patrick Gavin, "Bryce Harper Goes to Bat for AFL-CIO," Politico, May 2, 2013. www.politico.com.
35. Quoted in Bill Ordine, "Sportsperson of the Year: Mo Gaba," Pressbox, July 28, 2020. https://pressboxonline.com.

Chapter Three: Superstar Support

36. Quoted in Scott Stump, "Nathan Chen Says Gold Medal Wouldn't Be Possible Without One Person: His Mom," *Today*, February 10, 2022. www.today.com.
37. Quoted in Stump, "Nathan Chen Says Gold Medal Wouldn't Be Possible Without One Person."
38. Quoted in Sarah Duren, "'That's My Baby!' Converse Family Heading to Super Bowl to Watch Tre Flowers Play with the Bengals," KENS 5 News, February 13, 2022. www.kens5.com.
39. Quoted in Alan Abrahamson, "Abrahamson: Caeleb Dressel Wins Olympics with Tear-Jerking Video Call After Gold," NBC Olympics, October 8, 2021. www.nbcolympics.com.
40. Quoted in Amulya Shekhar, "'You Da Real MVP': When Kevin Durant Gave the Greatest NBA MVP Acceptance Speech of All Time 7 Years Ago," The SportsRush, June 6, 2021. https://thesportsrush.com.
41. Quoted in SportsNet, "McDavid on Winning Art Ross Trophy: Wouldn't Be Here Without My Teammates," April 10, 2017. www.sportsnet.ca.
42. Quoted in Alessandro Poggi, "Mikaela Shiffrin Leaves Beijing 2022 Without a Medal: 'My Teammates Are What Carried Me Through This Olympics,'" Olympics, February 20, 2022. https://olympics.com.
43. Quoted in Brandon Austin, "Former Pro Bowler LeSean McCoy Reveals Why Tom Brady Is the Greatest Teammate Ever: 'What He Says, You Believe It,'" Sportscasting, January 13, 2022. www.sportscasting.com.
44. Quoted in Dodgers Nation, "Dodgers: Kenley Jansen Talks Clubhouse Atmosphere Under Dave Roberts," 2019. www.dodgersnation.com.
45. Quoted in Vaughn McClure, "NFL Quarterbacks Coaches Play Crucial Role, Just Ask Matt Ryan," ESPN, July 25, 2018. www.espn.com.
46. Quoted in Mansi Jain, "Michael Phelps Sends a Special Message to Coach AKA Dad Figure on Father's Day for Monumental Win," EssentiallySports, June 20, 2022. www.essentiallysports.com.
47. Quoted in Jason Smith, "How to Tell If Your Athlete Is Coachable," *USA Today*, June 12, 2018. https://usatodayhss.com.
48. Quoted in Shi Davidi, "In Good Hands," Sportsnet, 2018. www.sportsnet.ca.
49. Quoted in *People*, "Top NBA Trainer Shares the Diet and Fitness Rules His Athletes Live By," December 8, 2020. https://people.com.

50. Mike Trout (@MikeTrout), "I am grateful to have coaches, teammates, family & a wife who continue to support me so I can play the game I love," Twitter, November 14, 2019, 7:37 p.m. https://twitter.com.

Chapter Four: Seizing Opportunities

51. Quoted in Brent Schrotenboer, "Inside the Drive That Won Super Bowl 56 for the Los Angeles Rams," Yahoo! News, February 14, 2022. https://news.yahoo.com.
52. Quoted in Keith Langlois, "'I Want the Ball in My Hands'—Crunch-Time Cade Leads Pistons to Summer League Win," NBA, August 13, 2021. www.nba.com.
53. Quoted in Howard Balzer, "'Surreal' the Best Way to Describe Kurt Warner's Career," *Sports Illustrated*, July 2, 2020. www.si.com.
54. Quoted in Marcia Smith, "Little Wes Welker Set to Come Up Big for Patriots," *Orange County Register* (Irvine, CA), January 29, 2008. www.ocregister.com.
55. Quoted in Bob Klapisch, "Stories of Derek Jeter's Greatness from All Corners of Captain Clutch's Career," Bleacher Report, January 21, 2020. https://bleacherreport.com.
56. Quoted in Sean Gregory, "American Snowboard Phenom Chloe Kim Is Already a Huge Star at the Winter Olympics. Her Next Goal? The School Prom," *Time*, February 9, 2018. https://time.com.
57. Quoted in Jordan Davidson, "5 Sports Heroes Explain How They Calmed Their Nerves When the Stakes Were High," *Men's Health*, November 30, 2016. www.menshealth.com.
58. Quoted in Davidson, "5 Sports Heroes Explain How They Calmed Their Nerves When the Stakes Were High."
59. Quoted in Troy Hanning, "Why Tim Duncan Was the Best Leader in NBA History," Basketball Network, January 29, 2022. www.basketballnetwork.net.
60. Quoted in Shannon Ryan, "What Candace Parker Is Teaching Teammate Kaleah Copper and WNBA's Next Generation," *The Athletic*, July 7, 2022. https://theathletic.com.
61. Quoted in Joshua Emerson Smith and Beto Alvarez, "Focus: Turning Skateboarding into a Global Culture," *San Diego (CA) Union-Tribune*, July 1, 2016. www.mcall.com.
62. "Make-A-Wish Celebrates John Cena for Granting Record 500 Wishes," WWE Community. https://community.wwe.com.
63. Quoted in Goodreads, "*No Limits* Quotes," 2022. www.goodreads.com.

ORGANIZATIONS TO CONTACT

National Collegiate Athletic Association (NCAA)
www.ncaa.org
The NCAA oversees college athletics for men and women at all levels. On its website, the NCAA maintains schedules and links to member institutions, as well as stories about athletes, programs, and various schools. There are also resources to help teen athletes make the most of their high school athletic and academic careers.

TeensHealth: Sports Center
https://kidshealth.org/en/teens/sports-center
This website from Nemours, which provides information about all aspects of health, focuses on sports and fitness information for teens. There are articles about training, sports injuries, sports psychology, choosing the right sport, and preparing for the next season.

US Department of Agriculture: Eating for Exercise and Sports
www.nutrition.gov/topics/basic-nutrition/eating-exercise-and-sports
This US Department of Agriculture site contains links to articles and resources about sports nutrition, supplements, and health guidelines for athletes of all ages. In particular, there is information about fueling young athletes for peak performance during practices and competitions.

US Olympic and Paralympic Committee (USOPC)
www.teamusa.org
The USOPC represents all US Olympic teams and athletes. Its website contains the latest news on competitions and stories about athletes and previous Olympic Games. There are also articles explaining the rules and histories of every Olympic sport, as well as resources for how to get involved in local leagues and clubs.

FOR FURTHER RESEARCH

Books

Jeremy Bhandari, *Trust the Grind: How World Class Athletes Got to the Top*. Miami, FL: Mango, 2020.

Troy Horne and Moses Horne, *Mental Toughness for Young Athletes: Eight Proven 5-Minute Mindset Exercises for Kids and Teens Who Play Competitive Sports*. Lakewood, CO: Buggily Group, 2020.

Rachel Ignotofsky, *Women in Sports: 50 Fearless Athletes Who Played to Win*. Berkeley, CA: Ten Speed, 2017.

Kyleigh Villarreal, *More than a Game: 13 Keys to Success for Teen Athletes on and off the Field*. Fenton, MO: Together Change Happens, 2016.

Internet Sources

Dan Abrahams, "How to Be a Consistently Great Soccer Player," *Soccer Today*, September 10, 2020. www.soccertoday.com.

Cleveland Clinic Staff, "Athletes and Mental Health: Breaking the Stigma," Cleveland Clinic. https://health.clevelandclinic.org.

Jackie MacMullan, "Rise Above It or Drown: How Elite NBA Athletes Handle Pressure," ESPN, May 29, 2019. www.espn.com.

Alyson Meister and Maude Lavanchy, "Athletes Are Shifting the Narrative Around Mental Health at Work," *Harvard Business Review*, September 24, 2021. https://hbr.org.

Korin Miller, "3 Pro Athletes Share Their Workout Secrets—and the Surprising Ways They Stay Motivated," *Runner's World*, December 16, 2021. www.runnersworld.com.

Princeton Review, "How to Get Athletic Scholarships," 2022. www.princetonreview.com.

TeensHealth, "Choosing the Right Sport for You," 2021. https://kidshealth.org.

Trine University, "Mental Toughness: The Key to Athletic Success," Center for Sports Studies blog, 2021. www.trine.edu.

INDEX

Note: Boldface page numbers indicate illustrations.

agents, 38
Allman, Valarie, 16–17

Basketball Insiders (website), 16
Berra, Yogi, 19
Biles, Simone, 8, **9**, 52
Bird, Sue, 14–15, 35
Bleacher Report (website), 14
Bowman, Bob, 39
Brady, Tom, **13**, 13–14, 36
Burrow, Joe, 22–23

Cena, John, 50–51, **51**
charity/volunteer work, 50–51
Chen, Nathan, 30, 31, **31**
composure, 23–25
confidence, 21
Cooper, Travis, 12–13
Copper, Kahleah, 48
Cunningham, Cade, 41–42
Curry, Stephen, 4–5, **7**, 34, 40, 46

Daily Mail (newspaper), 19
Department of Agriculture, US: Eating for Exercise and Sports (website), 57
Diggins, Jessie, 22
Djokovic, Novak, 28
Dressel, Caeleb, 32–33
Dressel, Meghan, 33
Duncan, Tim, 47–48
Durant, Kevin, 33–34

eating disorders, 22
Elway, John, 37–38

Felix, Allyson, 24
Florio, Mike, 38
Flowers, Crystal, 32
Flowers, Rodney, 32
Flowers, Tre, 32
focus, 22–23
Fouts, Dan, 47
Fox, John, **20**, 21

Goodell, Roger, 11
GQ (magazine), 12
Green, Draymond, 6

Harper, Bryce, 29
Harrison, James, 44, 47
Harvard Magazine, 9
Hawk, Tony, 49–50
Huffman, Nikki, 40
Hutchinson, Aidan, 11

Indianapolis Star (newspaper), 21

Jacobellis, Lindsey, 11
James, LeBron, 28, 40, 42
Jansen, Kenley, 37
Jeter, Derek, 45
Jordan, Michael, 26

Kerr, Steve, 5
Kershaw, Clayton, 37
Kim, Chloe, 14, 45–46
Kupp, Cooper, 41
Kwan, Michelle, 47

Lawrence, Trevor, 18
leadership, 47–50
Ledecky, Katie, 17
Lee, Suni, 22
Los Angeles Dodgers, 37
Los Angeles Times (newspaper), 12
losses, learning from, 25–26

Mahomes, Jackson, **33**

Mahomes, Pat, **33**
Mahomes, Patrick, 10, **33**
Mahomes, Randi, **33**
Make-A-Wish Foundation, 50
Mancini, Trey, 26–27, 29
Manning, Peyton, **20**, 20–21
Martinez, J.D., **15**
McCoy, LeSean, 36
McDavid, Connor, 34
McLaughlin, Sydney, 23
McVay, Sean, 41
meditation, 28
Men's Health (magazine), 10, 46
mental health, 22, 52
mental toughness
  components of, 19–21
  developing, 29
  response to pressure and, 44
Morehouse, Tim, 46–47
Morgan, Alex, 34, **36**
Murray, Kyler, 12

National Collegiate Athletic Association (NCAA), 57
Newell, Elliott, 21
NFL Europe, 42
No Limits (Michael Phelps), 52
nutritionists, 35

off-season training, 13–14, 16
Oladipo, Victor, 21
Olajuwon, Hakeem, 12
Olympic and Paralympic Committee, US (USOPC), 57
O'Neill, Paul, 45
Orgeron, Ed, 22–23

Parker, Candace, 48, 49
Parker, Tony, 48
Payne, Brandon, 5
Pederson, Joc, 37
Phelps, Debbie, 39
Phelps, Michael, 8, 22, 39, 52
ProFootballTalk (blog), 38
Pulisic, Christian, 17–18

Rapinoe, Megan, 34, **36**
Ravin, Idan, 40
resilience, 26–28
Rivers, Glenn "Doc," 39
Roberts, Dave "Doc," 37
Ross, Terrence, 16

San Diego Union-Tribune (newspaper), 50
Seager, Corey, 37
SELF (magazine), 14
Shape (magazine), 14

Shiffrin, Mikaela, 35
Skatepark Project (Tony Hawk Foundation), 50
skills training, 15–18
So You Think You Can Dance (TV program), 16
Sports Illustrated (magazine), 42
Stafford, Matthew, 41, **43**
Stark, Melissa, 11
Stroupe, Bobby, 10
Suguiyama, Yuri, 17
support
    from coaches, 36–39
    sources of, 30–34
    sports trainers and, 39–40
    from teammates, 34–36
Swimming World (magazine), 17

TeensHealth: Sports Center (website), 57
Thomas, Gabby, 9
Thompson, Klay, 34
Time (magazine), 23
Today (TV program), 30
Tolbert, Kebba, 9
Tony Hawk Foundation (Skatepark Project), 50
Tony Hawk's Pro Skater (video game), 50

trainers, 39–40
Travis, Devon, 39–40
Trout, Mike, 40

volunteer work, 50–51
Vonn, Lindsey, **27**, 27–28

Walsh, Vincent, 19–20
Warner, Kurt, 42–43

Washington Post (newspaper), 17
Watt, JJ, 50
Welker, Wes, 44, 47
Williams, Serena, **24**, 25–26, 42
Wilson, Russell, 28
Women's Health (magazine), 35

PICTURE CREDITS

Cover: Brocreative/Shutterstock.com

- 7: Associated Press
- 9: Simone Ferraro/Alamy Stock Photo
- 13: ZUMA Press/Alamy Stock Photo
- 15: Gerry Angus/Icon Sportswire DCA/Gerry Angus/Icon Sportswire/Newscom
- 20: Tribune Content Agency LLC/Alamy Stock Photo
- 24: PA Images/Alamy Stock Photo
- 27: PA Images/Alamy Stock Photo
- 31: ZUMA Press, Inc./Alamy Stock Photo
- 33: Associated Press
- 36: Xinhua/Alamy Stock Photo
- 43: Associated Press
- 49: SPP Sports Press Photo/Alamy Stock Photo
- 51: MediaPunch Inc/Alamy Stock Photo

ABOUT THE AUTHOR

After graduating from the University of Oregon, James Roland became a newspaper reporter, primarily focused on education. He later became a magazine writer and editor as well as an author of more than a dozen books. He and his wife, Heidi, have three children, Chris, Alexa, and Carson.